READING CORNER

PHONICS

The Great Soup Mystery

Written by
Clare De Marco

Illustrated by
Andy Rowland

Practising long vowel phonemes,
trisyllabic words and tricky words

First published in 2010 by
Franklin Watts
338 Euston Road
London NW1 3BH

Franklin Watts Australia
Hachette Children's Books
Level 17/207 Kent Street
Sydney NSW 2000

Text © Clare De Marco 2010
Illustration © Andy Rowland 2010

A CIP catalogue record for this book
is available from the British Library.

ISBN: 978 0 7496 9172 1 (hbk)
ISBN: 978 0 7496 9181 3 (pbk)

Series Editor: Jackie Hamley
Series Advisors: Dr Barrie Wade,
 Dr Hilary Minns
Series Designer: Jonathan Hair

Printed in China

Franklin Watts is a division of
Hachette Children's Books,
an Hachette UK company
www.hachette.co.uk

There is a puzzle at the end of this book.
Here are the answers for you to check later!

The matching words are:
meat feet, meet, seat
bread fed, head, red
honey funny, money, runny
bowl foal, goal, hole

One morning, Mr Brown
made a pan of soup.

"This should be nice,"
he thought. "It's full of
meat and herbs."

5

When the soup was ready,
he put it near the kitchen
window to cool.

7

Then there was a knock
at the door.

8

"Hello!" said the farmer.
"My bees have made lots of
honey. Would you like some?"

9

"Yes, please," said Mr Brown.

"Would you like a bowl of soup?"

"Thank you," said the farmer.

Mr Brown went to fetch the soup.
"That's odd," he thought.
"I'm sure there was more."

13

He gave the farmer his bowl of
soup. Then he went inside.

15

Soon there was a knock
at the door.

16

"Hello!" said the baker. "My daughter has made too much bread. Would you like a loaf?"

"Yes, please," said Mr Brown.

"Would you like a bowl of soup?"

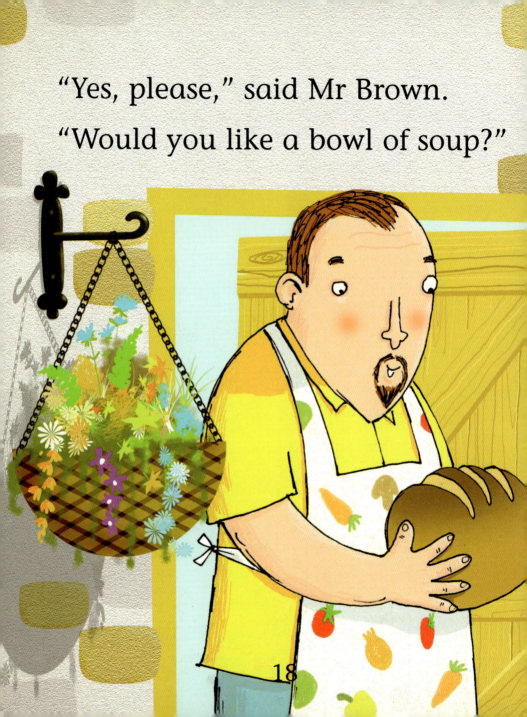

"Thank you," said the baker.

Mr Brown went to fetch the soup.

"What a mystery!" he thought.

"There isn't much left!"

21

He gave the baker her bowl
of soup. Then he went inside.

23

"There's nothing left!" he cried.
Then he saw a spoon,
and a head.

25

"Nice soup, Mr Brown," said Mrs Brown.

"You're the soup thief!" laughed Mr Brown.

27

"Sorry!" said Mrs Brown.

"Never mind," said Mr Brown.
"I can have some bread and
honey instead!"

29

Puzzle Time!

Match the words that rhyme
to the pictures.

meat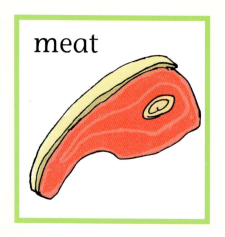

fed

money

hole

feet

bread

funny

foal

honey

meet

goal

head

red

bowl

runny

seat

See page 2 for answers.

Notes for parents and teachers

READING CORNER PHONICS has been structured to provide maximum support for children learning to read through synthetic phonics. The stories are designed for independent reading but may also be used by adults for sharing with young children.

The teaching of early reading through synthetic phonics focuses on the 44 sounds in the English language, and how these sounds correspond to their written form in the 26 letters of the alphabet. Carefully controlled vocabulary makes these books accessible for children at different stages of phonics teaching, progressing from simple CVC (consonant-vowel-consonant) words such as "top" (t-o-p) to trisyllabic words such as "messenger" (mess-en-ger). READING CORNER PHONICS allows children to read words in context, and also provides visual clues and repetition to further support their reading. These books will help develop the all important confidence in the new reader, and encourage a love of reading that will last a lifetime!

If you are reading this book with a child, here are a few tips:

1. Talk about the story before you start reading. Look at the cover and the title. What might the story be about? Why might the child like it?

2. Encourage the child to reread the story, and to retell the story in their own words, using the illustrations to remind them what has happened.

3. Discuss the story and see if the child can relate it to their own experience, or perhaps compare it to another story they know.

4. Give praise! Small mistakes need not always be corrected. If a child is stuck on a word, ask them to try and sound it out and then blend it together again, or model this yourself. For example "wish" w-i-sh "wish".

READING CORNER PHONICS covers two grades of synthetic phonics teaching, with three levels at each grade. Each level has a certain number of words per story, indicated by the number of bars on the spine of the book:

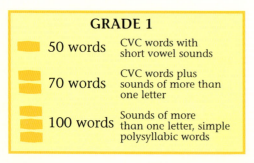

GRADE 1

50 words — CVC words with short vowel sounds

70 words — CVC words plus sounds of more than one letter

100 words — Sounds of more than one letter, simple polysyllabic words

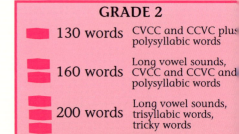

GRADE 2

130 words — CVCC and CCVC plus polysyllabic words

160 words — Long vowel sounds, CVCC and CCVC and polysyllabic words

200 words — Long vowel sounds, trisyllabic words, tricky words